J Staunt
Staunton, Ted, 1956-
Morgan gets cracking /
4232

34028084782649
FM  $5.95  ocn794300901
03/05/14

4232

P9-CLV-069
4028 08478 2649
HARRIS COUNTY PUBLIC LIBRARY

WITHDRAWN

# Morgan Gets Cracking

## Ted Staunton

Illustrated by Bill Slavin

Formac Publishing Company Limited
Halifax

Text copyright © 2012 by Ted Staunton
Illustrations copyright © 2012 by Bill Slavin
First published in the United States in 2013.

All rights reserved. No part of this book may be reproduced or transmitted in
any form or by any means, electronic or mechanical, including photocopying,
or by any information or storage or retrieval system, without permission in
writing from the publisher.

Formac Publishing Company Limited recognizes the support of the Province of
Nova Scotia through the Department of Communities, Culture and Heritage.
We are pleased to work in partnership with the Culture Division to develop
and promote our culture resources for all Nova Scotians. We acknowledge
the financial support of the Government of Canada through the Canada Book
Fund for our publishing activities. We acknowledge the support of the Canada
Council for the Arts which last year invested $24.3 million in writing and
publishing throughout Canada.

**Library and Archives Canada Cataloguing in Publication**

Staunton, Ted, 1956-
    Morgan gets cracking / Ted Staunton ; illustrated by Bill Slavin.

(First novels)
Issued also in electronic formats.
ISBN 978-1-4595-0075-4 (bound).--ISBN 978-1-4595-0074-7 (pbk.)

    I. Slavin, Bill  II. Title.  III. Series: First novels

PS8587.T334M664 2012          jC813'.54          C2012-902939-4

Formac Publishing Company Limited    Distributed in the United States by:
5502 Atlantic Street    Orca Book Publishers
Halifax, NS,    P.O. Box 468
Canada B3H 1G4    Custer, WA U.S.A.
www.formac.ca    98240-0468

Printed and bound in
Manufactured by Friesens Corporation in Altona, Manitoba, Canada in
August 2012.
Job #77083

# Table of Contents

# 1

# Chicken Big

Aldeen Hummel is like a chicken.

I don't mean she *is* a chicken: Aldeen is the Godzilla of Grade Three. But she's also like a chicken. I never thought of this before, but our class has never gone on a field trip to a farm before, either. There are chickens all around us. They twitch and scuff the dirt while the farm lady talks; so does Aldeen. Their necks are long and their heads bob around; same with Aldeen. Okay, Aldeen has witchy hair and smudged up glasses, which are not like a chicken, but she does have a noogie knuckle that pecks as hard as a chicken beak. I know, because she's noogied me twice today.

The farm lady is showing us this big rack of eggs. It's making me hungry. I want to ask my dad what he made us for lunch. He's helping on our trip. Dad is way over by Mrs. Ross, our teacher.

Aldeen is beside me. Her head keeps jerking toward the new kid in our class, Curtis. Jerking is the right way to say it, too, because Curtis is a jerk. Curtis and his spiky hair came to our class three days ago

and all he's done so far is show off. First day, he showed off his karate moves until Mrs. Ross told him to stop. Second day, he showed off with his yo-yo. Today, on the bus, he kept showing off his cell phone and the games on it, until Mrs. Ross made him put it away. Curtis said he had to check for texts.

Right now, he's by the eggs, making bored faces at everyone while the farm lady talks. Kids are giggling. The farm lady doesn't notice. Mrs. Ross does. She looks around and Curtis turns into Mister Perfect. Mrs. Ross looks away. Curtis makes a face at her, too. I look at my best friend, Charlie. Charlie rolls his eyes. Beside me, I hear "*bek-bek-bek,*" like a chicken cluck. I look: it's Aldeen giggling.

Geez, Curtis isn't even funny.

Aldeen sees me looking. Her eyes go squinchy and her noogie knuckle comes up. Just then, the farm lady says, "Let's all go this way," and our class starts to move. Aldeen's knuckle goes down. *Whew.*

As soon as the grown-ups go by, Curtis says, "Watch and be amazed!" He scoops up three eggs. You're not supposed to touch them. Then he starts to juggle. We all stop and stare. The eggs sail up and around. Curtis really can juggle; it *is* amazing.

Then Curtis says, "This is so easy it's boring. Here, catch Aldeen." And *zoop, zoop, zoop,* the three eggs sail at Aldeen Hummel. *Splat. Splat. Splat.* Before you can squawk, Aldeen is covered with egg.

There is total silence. Then Mrs. Ross's voice sounds behind us: "Aldeen! *What* are you doing?"

# 2

# Super Noogies

You don't mess with the Godzilla of Grade Three. Will Aldeen push Curtis into the pig pen? Stuff him into a pumpkin? Stampede cows over him? Nope, nope and nope. Aldeen bumps Kaely into a puddle, squishes Mark's lunch and knocks over the apples.

When we finally pile on the bus she noogies me and growls, "Move over."

"Hey," I rub my arm, "I'm saving this seat for Charlie."

"Tough bananas." Her knuckle pops up. I move. Aldeen plops down and starts scraping the bottom of her running shoe on the back of the seat in front of us. Something smells bad. I look at what she's scraping off her shoe. I remember the cows and how they ... I can't get the window open. Dad can't either. "Won't be long," he says. "What smells in here?"

"You smelt it, you dealt it," Curtis says from across the aisle. Dad looks around. Aldeen noogies me again as if it's my fault. There are still egg bits on her glasses. Why does she have to sit here?

When we get back to school, moms and dads are waiting. Aldeen's granny is by the cab she drives, smoking a little cigar. Beside it is a red sports car with its top down. A tanned guy in surf shorts and sunglasses is juggling a soccer ball. He heads it so it goes behind him, then he kicks it with his heel so it sails back over his shoulder again.

"Who's that?" Charlie says.

"Haven't you met Superman?" says Curtis. "My father."

"Let's say hi," says Dad. We go over. Superman kicks the ball to Curtis. Curtis dekes around Charlie. Charlie goes after him; he's good at soccer.

My dad introduces us. "Cal," says Superman, shaking Dad's hand. He puts his sunglasses on top of his head and looks even cooler.

"Quite the car," says Aldeen's granny, leaning against her cab.

"Summer only," says Superman. "Have to get out the Hummer for winter soon."

"For sure." Aldeen's granny blows out cigar smoke. It drifts towards Superman's face. He waves it away and puts his shades back down.

My dad is rubbing his shaking hand as if it hurts. "Nice to meet you," he says. "Ready, Morgan?"

Behind us comes, "AHHH!" I look. Aldeen is rubbing her butt. She kicks the soccer ball away. Curtis is laughing. His hair hasn't moved at all.

"Man, I have good aim," says Curtis.

This is it, I think. Instead, Aldeen shoves *me* out of the way and stomps to the cab.

"If you want," Curtis says to me, "I'll teach you how to box."

# 3

# A Safe Mix

After supper, Dad and I bake. There is a neighbourhood party on Saturday and Dad is in charge of the dessert table. Mom is helping with games. She goes to the mall to get stuff for that, while we make cupcakes.

I like baking — especially if I get to scoop nibbles from the mixing bowl.

After, as we clean up, I pick three eggs out of the carton. If Curtis can do it, maybe I can too. Back when I was new kid in our class, I said I could juggle. And play bass guitar and do magic. I couldn't do any of it. Well, I did magic trick Aldeen once by making a dime disappear, but that was by accident. I haven't thought about that stuff in a long time.

I have three eggs and two hands. How do you start? By throwing them all in the air, I guess. Dad is at the sink. I get set to toss. Dad says, "Watcha doing, sport?"

I stop. "Ummm ... Juggling?" I feel silly.

Dad looks at me. He looks at the eggs. Then he says, "Just a sec." He leaves the kitchen. A minute later Dad calls me to the living room. He's at the couch. He's holding three socks. He squishes each one up into its stretchy part to make three little lumps. "Watch," he says. He has two lumps in one hand and one in the other. He tosses one of the two in the air, then the one from the other hand, and as the first starts to fall he tosses the third one. He's juggling!

"Cool!" I say. I still have the eggs. I put them on a chair and move closer to watch. Dad drops a sock. It lands on the couch. "Your turn," he says. He shows me how to start with two lumps. "Socks don't break," he says, "And if you practice over the couch you don't have to pick them up off the floor." I try it. It's tricky even with two. "Why do you want to juggle?" Dad asks.

"Curtis did it today," I say, "At the farm. Then he egged Aldeen."

"Hmm," Dad says. "Why am I not surprised? Here's another little tip. If you ever *do* juggle with eggs, make sure they're hard-boiled, huh?"

I drop a few socks. Dad says "Good," anyway.

"Will Curtis be at the neighbourhood party?" I ask.

"I don't think so," Dad says, "Where do they live?"

I shrug. "I don't think I want to know," I say.

"I think I get what you mean," Dad says. He rubs his hand again.

The front door opens. Mom comes in with a shopping bag. "Guess who I ran into at the mall?" she says. "And invited to the neighbourhood party?"

I drop the socks. Dad starts to sink into the chair. Then he stops — and picks up the eggs. Then he sinks.

# 4

# The Winning Goal

"My guitar is a Stratocaster," Curtis is saying, "And my amp is as big as ..."

I don't care how big it is. It's only lunch time and I'm already sick of Curtis. "Maybe I'll bring it to the party," he's saying, "Then I'll have something to do."

Oh, man. Why did Curtis have to come to our table? Charlie and I sat here first to try and get away from him and now there's no place left to move. We're stuck here at the table until the bell for going outside rings.

Beside me, Aldeen is pounding up her cookies in a baggie. I don't know why; I'm just glad it's cookies, not me. Curtis is still blah, blah, blahing. How can I at least stop listening? I stick my hands in my pockets. There's money there; I had to buy milk today. I pull it out: three dimes. I have an idea. "Hey, Charlie," I say across the table, "Want to play finger hockey?"

Finger hockey is a game where one player hooks his first finger and little finger onto the table top. That's the goal. Then the other player dumps the dimes onto the table. You have to flick one dime between the other two with each shot to work across the table and shoot on goal. If you miss shooting between the other two, or your shot on goal, it's the other player's turn. I taught everyone how to play, back when I was new kid.

"Sure," says Charlie. We clear away our lunch stuff. I make the goal first. Charlie shakes the dimes and dumps them on the table. *Flick, flick, flick*, he goes. He takes a last shot, at my goal. It goes wide and the dime falls off the table.

My turn. Charlie makes the goal with his fingers. *Flick, flick, flick, flick*. My last shot ends up short.

Charlie's turn. His second shot doesn't go between the other dimes. My turn: this time I score in three flicks. "Yessss!"

"That's so easy," says Curtis.

"Oh yeah?" I say, "Want to try?"

"Sure," he says.

Finger hockey isn't as easy as it looks, and I'm pretty good at it. It's the only game I can beat Charlie at. Maybe I've found something to beat Show-Off Man Curtis at too. I look at Charlie. He smiles and lets Curtis take his place. Curtis is shaking up the dimes when, "Move over, tubby," Aldeen pushes me out of the way. "It's my turn."

"Wha —?" I say. It's too late. Aldeen is kneeling down and making a finger goal. Curtis starts flicking the dimes. Aldeen leans in. Her face is right down at the edge of the table. Her eyes are squinched and her mouth is hanging open, she's

watching so hard. Curtis lines up one last shot. He flicks, hard. The dime zooms across the table, misses the goal, and sails into Aldeen's mouth instead. I hear a gulp. Aldeen swallows the dime.

# 5

# Gulp

Curtis jumps up, pointing and hooting, "She swallowed it, she swallowed it! What a shot! You owe me a dime, Big Mouth!"

And then something amazing happens. For the first time in the whole history of the world, kids start laughing at Aldeen Hummel. Hummel the Bummel. Queen of Mean. The Godzilla of Grade Three.

Aldeen turns as purple as her sweat suit. This time for sure, I think. She spins around to me. "It's your fault, Morgan." She whacks me with her bag of cookies, grabs her stuff and stomps out of the lunch room.

Oh-oh time. It doesn't matter that it's not my fault, if Aldeen says it is. Plus, she is coming to my house after school, like she always does when her mom and granny are both at work. There's no escape.

Sure enough, first thing she says on the way to my place is, "You owe me a dime."

"I do not. It was my dime."

"Yeah, but I swallowed it, so I didn't get to keep it." Aldeen glares as if it's my fault.

"You weren't *supposed* to get to keep it."

Up pops Aldeen's noogie knuckle. Why even argue? When we get to my place I get money out of my piggy bank. Aldeen takes it and goes to talk to Mom. She's in the kitchen getting us a snack. I start for the kitchen but then I see Aldeen's backpack by the door. It's even messier than Aldeen's hair, and a paper is sticking out of it. I can see part of a picture. Aldeen is good at art, so I sneak a peek. It's a pencil crayon drawing of a guy. He's pretty busy; I think he's supposed to be juggling and kicking a soccer ball at the same time and he's got a guitar strapped on and a superhero cape. He's wearing clothes like the ones Curtis had on. And he has Curtis's spiky yellow hair. And ... Oh no, I think it *is* Curtis.

I figured if Aldeen was going to draw him she'd give him horns and a tail. She made him a superhero. What's going on? Aldeen doesn't *like* Curtis, does she? How could she? Besides, Aldeen doesn't like anybody. But imagine if they teamed up: Godzilla and Show-Off Man. The back of my neck goes as prickly as Curtis's hair. Aldeen *can't* like Curtis. Can she?

What happens if she does?

# 6

# Party at Home Plate

On Saturday the sun is shining hot and our street turns into a party. There's music playing and lots of people. There's a bouncy castle. Dad and some other grown-ups are getting the food tables ready. I've already picked all the desserts I want to try after I have burgers and dogs. Curtis's dad Superman is doing the barbequing. He brought along a gas grill almost as big as the Hummer he hauled it in.

All of us kids are playing soccer baseball. Mom and Aldeen's granny are umpires. I mean, almost all of us are playing: Curtis is just watching. "If I kick too many home runs, I'll get my new runners dirty," he says, taking out his cell phone. "Hippo Hunt is more fun, anyway." He starts playing his game. At least he didn't bring his electric guitar.

Right now, I'm panting at second base. I just kicked a double. Charlie's on third base. If Aldeen boots a good one and I score, our team will win. Winners get first burgers. The ball rolls at Aldeen. I get set to run. Aldeen winds up, her face smooshes like an accordion, and bammo,

she nails the ball way down past the fire hydrant.

I race for home. Aldeen runs so fast she almost passes me. Everybody cheers as we cross home plate. I'm huffing too hard to say much, but Aldeen yells, "Hey Curtis, did ya see that?"

Curtis looks up from his cell phone. He makes his lips flat and sighs, "Wow, Aldeen." Then he slow motion claps with one finger of each hand.

Aldeen turns away. Her face is red from running. I turn too — toward the food. I want a cold pop and a burger and —

"Okay kids," Mom calls, "Last game before food. And we saved best for last: water balloon toss! Winners get first dessert."

I'm hungry and thirsty but I'm hot and sweaty too. I think how nice it would feel to get a great big cool splash. *Aaaah*.

And then I know what would feel even better: to soak Curtis.

# 7

# Scramble

I can see it now: Curtis soaking wet, down
to his new runners, with red balloon stuck
to his face, his dumb spiked hair all flat, and
water running out of his cell phone. *Oh,
yeah.* Aldeen's granny is calling, "Everybody
get a partner!" All I have to do is get Curtis
for my partner and blast him, first throw.

Then someone grabs my arm. It's

Charlie. "C'mon, Morg," he says, "We can win this and get first dessert too."

"But —" I say. But how can I say no to my best friend, even if it is to get Curtis? I look over and it doesn't matter anyway: Aldeen is dragging Curtis towards her granny. Oh well, maybe she has the same idea. I turn to Charlie. "Let's do it!" I say. We high five and head over.

There's a problem. The grown-ups are all saying, "Well, I thought *you* got them." It turns out there aren't any balloons. I'm just about to go be first in line for food when Aldeen's granny says, "Well, let's do it the old-fashioned way. Who's got some eggs? We can toss them instead."

Charlie's mom says, "I've got a dozen in the fridge. I'll get them."

"Balloon toss with eggs?" someone says, "Ewwwww." I think, *Excellent.*

I have just had the best idea of my whole life. It will get me first dessert and mess up Curtis at the same time. "I'll be right back," I tell Charlie.

Then I sneak over to the salads table and slip a hard-boiled egg into my pocket.

# 8

# Cooking Something Up

By the time I get back, Charlie's mom is back too. I don't see the eggs. Right now she's uncoiling a hose. Mom gathers us around and explains the game. "Okay. Partners line up facing each other, three paces apart. Each pair gets a raw egg."

"*Ewwwwwww.*"

Mom says, "When I say go, toss the

egg to your partner. If they make the catch, you both take a step back and your partner throws to you, and so on. If your egg breaks —"

"*Ewwwwwwwww*"

"— You're out. You're also a mess. Luckily we have a hose handy. Last partners throwing win. Okay everybody, pair up and line up."

Someone has to go pee. Someone wants their hat. Charlie needs to tie his shoes. Curtis has to give his cell phone to his dad. Now's my chance. I run to Aldeen. "Listen," I puff, "You can get Curtis back for all the jerky stuff he's done to you. Tell him you've got a hard-boiled egg to throw, then heave the raw one at him. He'll think he's going to make a superstar catch, but you'll egg him

instead, just like he did to you. It's perfect! And if you do, I'll give you first dessert."

Aldeen pushes up her glasses. "How do you know you'll get first dessert?"

"Um, I've just got a feeling," I say.

"Hmmf," she says.

Curtis is coming back. "Do it!" I say. I run back to Charlie. Mom puts us in line. Everyone is still shuffling around. I look over: Aldeen is whispering to Curtis. "Ready?" calls Mom. Nope, Aldeen is gone somewhere. Now she's back.

"Okay," calls Mom.

"Wait!" Dad and Aldeen's granny squeeze in beside Charlie and me. "We want to play, too."

"Ohh-kayyy," calls Mom. "Why not? Everyone ready?"

"No! Wait for Curtis!" Aldeen calls. I look: now *Curtis* is gone somewhere.

"Now what?" sighs Charlie. He wipes his hands on his shorts.

"Probably so nervous he had to pee," I say. I'm not nervous. I've got a hard-boiled egg in my pocket.

Curtis strolls back from wherever he went, like a king or something. Charlie's mom goes and gets the egg carton from a picnic table. She opens it. "Oh," she says, "Didn't know one was gone." She counts us all. "Good, there's enough." She starts handing out eggs. When she gets to Charlie and me, I grab the egg before Charlie can and shove it in my pocket. When she moves on I reach back in and pull out the hard-boiled one instead. It's time to get first dessert, even if I do have to give it to Aldeen.

# 9

# The Yolk's On ...

"Go!" calls Mom. I toss to Charlie; he catches. We take a step back. Charlie tosses to me; I catch. We take a step back. I toss, Charlie tosses, I toss. Back, back, back, we go.

Down the line there's a yell, then another, then laughing, as people miss and get splattered. That's not going to happen to us, though. How can it when we're throwing a hard-boiled egg? I'm glad Dad gave me that tip about juggling. I one-hand the next catch. "Be careful, Morgan!" Charlie calls.

"No sweat," I laugh. We step back. Beside me, Aldeen's granny crows, "Got it, good throw!" and steps back. I wonder when Aldeen is going to egg Curtis.

There's more yelling as eggs break. How many teams are left? I toss the egg. Charlie has to run to make the catch. "Morg! Watch it!"

"It's okay," I call. I can't tell him about the hard-boiled egg right now. I wonder if I should tell him later. I mean, it's not as if we're really cheating, is it? I'm just doing it to get Curtis, and I'm going to give Aldeen first dessert. There's no time to think about it now. We step back. I look around. Dad makes a catch. Curtis and Aldeen are still tossing too. *When is she going to egg him?*

"Ready?" Charlie calls. He's way back by now. "Ready," I call. Charlie's tongue is sticking out between his teeth. He throws underhand, high and soft.

It's a great throw. It doesn't need to be, but still. I watch the egg float in toward me. I'll do a two-hander catch, right over my head. Here it comes, closer ... closer ... Watch it into your hands, Dad always says, when we play catch. I wiggle my fingers, reach up, aaaand ... now! I clap my hands and SPLAT, raw egg gloops all over my face.

"AAAGH," I yell, and as I do I see something through the dripping curtain of egg: Curtis catching, one handed. Then he brings his hands together and does something funny with them. It's hard to tell what, with goo in my eyes. Then he throws. I look at Aldeen. She smiles and lifts her hands. Egg explodes all over her too.

# 10

# The Wild Bounce

Aldeen screams. Curtis is laughing. Charlie is saying "Nice try, Morg," And I'm stunned. How could ...? I wipe my hands on my shorts. There's a lump in my pocket. Aw, noooo ... Something tells me I pulled out the wrong egg.

But something else is wrong, too. Aldeen is yelling, "Noooo! It was hard-boiled! It was hard-boiled!" *Whaaaat?*

Then there's cheering all around me. Dad and Aldeen's granny have won the egg toss. "Next time, blindfolded!" Aldeen's granny high fives Dad. Dad balances the egg on his nose.

I go over and Charlie's mom sprays goo off me with the hose. It feels so good it's almost worth getting egged.

"Chow time!" grown ups are calling. Oh well, we still won first burgers at soccer baseball. I also have a hard-boiled egg to eat. I get a plate and put my egg on it, then I join the line up for burgers right behind Charlie. Soccer baseball winners are supposed to be first, but guess who's at the front of the line?

"So, last throw I switch her hard-boiled egg for the raw one I took," Curtis snickers to Charlie, "And I whip it back and egg her all over again! Perfect or what?"

"Uh-huh," says Charlie. "Where'd you get a raw egg?"

"From the carton. Snuck over just before we started. That's why one was missing. The hard-boiled one's right here in my pocket." Curtis pats his shorts.

Charlie rolls his eyes. I know it's true but I can't help saying, "Yeah right, Curtis." After all, it should be him who's soaking right now, not me. As we step up to the giant grill, Curtis pulls an egg out of his pocket. "Watch and be amazed," he says. "Hey dad, may I borrow the Super skull?"

Superman grins and waves his burger flipper thingy. "Sure." He flips up his shades and bends toward Curtis. His hair is spiky today too.

Curtis raps. The shell cracks. Raw egg gloops all over Superman's head. He snaps up. "CURTIS! WHAT THE —"

Curtis's eyes go wide. He starts stammering, "But, but, but ..."

Egg drips down Superman's face. He does not look so super anymore. He looks really mad. Curtis keeps on stammering.

"Think I'll get a burger later," I say to Charlie.

"Yeah," he says.

Aldeen walks up. Her witchy hair is plastered flat, like mine. Bits of shell are still in it. "Bwhat dud thab jerg bu now?" she asks. Her mouth is full.

I tell her about Curtis and the egg on Superman's head. Aldeen swallows.

"Serves him right," she says. She lifts something to take another bite. It's a hard-boiled egg. Hey, wait a ... Did she ... *How?*

Before I can ask anything Aldeen says, "Let's go in the bouncy castle. I don't wanna hang around here, I wanna play with my friends."

I think it's oh-oh time again.

# More novels in the First Novels series!

**Think Again, Robyn**

Hazel Hutchins

Illustrated by Yvonne Cathcart

Robyn stands up to a bully, makes a new friend and gets caught up in the excitement of the big game!

**Morgan and the Dune Racer**
Ted Staunton
Illustrated by Bill Slavin

It's Morgan's birthday and all he wants is Charlie's remote-control toy no matter what it takes or who he hurts to get it.

**Lilly Traps the Bullies**
Brenda Bellingham
Illustrated by Clarke MacDonald

Lilly has to make a decision: choose between old friends and the gang of cool kids.